**W9-BSX-408**

# Saint Manuel, Martyr

## By Miguel de Unamuno

Translated by Marciano Guerrero

1/25/2013

# Miguel de Unamuno (1864-1936)
# Saint Manuel, Martyr

## Brief Bio

Unamuno lived half of his life in the 19th century and the other half in the 20th. A Spanish man —Basque— of letters quite accomplished in many fields: poetry, drama, novel, essays, philosophy, politics, and foreign languages. He was professor of Greek at University of Salamanca from 1891, becoming its rector later on. Influenced by American philosopher William James and Danish philosopher Kierkegaard he developed an existentialist Christian theology, based on a tragic view of life and immortality. In 1936 he was dismissed from Salamanca for espousing the Allied cause in World War I and later for denouncing Francisco Franco's Falangists.

## Saint Manuel, Martyr

In some translations the novel is entitled *Saint Emmanuel the Good, Martyr*. I prefer a shorter title: *Saint Manuel, Martyr*. This brief novel is a framed novel in which Angela

### Saint Manuel, Martyr

Carballino (the narrator), a woman in her fifties, presents the story as her memoir. The memoir chronicles the spiritual experiences of Don Manuel, the priest of a remote mountain village called Valverde de Lucerna. Angela —the narrator— reveals Don Manuel's true feelings about his religion; that is, his loss of faith in God.

*Saint Manuel, Martyr* explores deep religious and philosophical paradoxes that question the meaning of life and death. In sum, the novel portrays a simple man without faith, who in his solitude, loneliness, and suffering *sees* that faith is merely an illusion, a dream that the common man dreams to fend off the terrible truth that only the brotherhood and nature in this world counts—that there's no otherworldly eternity. His life, then, is a deliberate fraud to console his parishioners.

### Major Works

Unamuno's *The Tragic Sense of Life* (1913) together with his novels *Mist,* and *San Manuel Martyr* have been universally acclaimed as the textbooks for Christian existentialism. *The Christ of Velázquez)* (1920) — is a religious poem in which Unamuno analyzes the figure of

Saint Manuel, Martyr
Christ to attempt to find a Christian source of redemption.

*If with this life only in view we have had
hope in Christ, we are of all men the most
to be pitied.*

**Saint Paul: I COR. 15:19.**

The bishop of the diocese of Renada, to which this my beloved village of Valverde de Lucerna belongs, is seeking (according to rumor), to initiate the process of beatification of our Don Manuel, or more correctly: San Manuel Bueno. San Manuel was parish priest here, I want to state in writing, by way of confession (although to what end only God, and not I can say), all that I can vouch for and remember of that matriarchal man who pervaded the most secret life of my soul, who was my true spiritual father, the father of my spirit, the spirit of myself, Angela Carballino.

The other father: my flesh-and-blood temporal father, I scarcely knew, having died when I was still a very young girl. I know that he came to Valverde de Lucerna from the outside world—that he was a stranger—and that he settled here when he married my mother. He had brought a number of books with him: *Don Quixote,* some plays from the classic theatre, some novels, a few histories, the *Bertoldo,* everything all mixed together. From these books (practically the only books in the whole village), I nurtured my young girl dreams, dreams which in turn devoured me.

My good mother told me very little either of the words or the deeds of my father.

All because the words and deeds of Don Manuel, whom she worshipped, of whom she was enamored, in common with all the rest of the village—in an exquisitely chaste manner, of course—had obliterated the memory of the words and deeds of her husband (my father), whom she commended to God, with full fervor, as she said her daily rosary.

Don Manuel I remember as if it were yesterday, from the time when I was a girl of ten years of age, just before I was taken to the convent school in the cathedral city of Renada. At that time Don Manuel —our saint— must have been about thirty-seven years old. He was tall, slender, and erect, carrying himself the way our bird Buitre Peak carries its crest, and his eyes had all the blue depth of our lake. As he walked he commanded all eyes, and not only the eyes but the hearts of all; gazing round at us he seemed to look through our flesh as through glass and penetrate our hearts.

All of us loved him, especially the children. And the things he said to us! Not words, things! The villagers could scent the odor of sanctity; they were intoxicated with it.

About this time my brother Lazarus, who was in America, from where he regularly sent us money with which we lived in decent leisure, asked my mother to send me to the convent school, so that my education might be completed outside the village. He suggested this move despite the fact that he had no special fondness for the nuns. "But since, as far as I know," he wrote us, "there are no lay schools there yet,—especially not for young ladies—we will have to make use of the ones that do exist. The important thing is for Angelita to receive some polish and not be forced to continue among village girls."

And so I entered the convent school.

At one point I even thought I would become a teacher; but pedagogy soon palled upon me.

At school I met girls from the city and I made friends with some of them. But I still kept in touch with people in our village, receiving frequent reports and sometimes a visit.

And the fame of the parish priest reached as far as the school, for he was beginning to be talked of in the cathedral city. The nuns never tired of asking me about him.

Ever since early youth I had been endowed, I don't very well know from where, with a large degree of curiosity and restlessness, due at least in part to that jumble of books which my father had collected, and these qualities were stimulated at school; especially in the course of a relationship which I developed with a girlfriend, who grew excessively attached to me. At times she proposed that we enter the same convent together, swearing to an everlasting "sisterhood"— and even that we seal the oath in blood. At other times she talked to me, with eyes half closed, of sweethearts and marriage adventures. Strangely enough, I have never heard from her since, or of what became of her, despite the fact that whenever our Don Manuel was spoken of, or when my mother wrote me something about him in her letters—which happened in almost every letter—and I read it to her, this girl would

4

exclaim, as if in rapture: "What luck, my dear, to be able to live near a saint like that, a live saint, of flesh and blood, and to be able to kiss his hand; when you go back to your village write me everything, everything, and tell me about him."

Five years passed at school, five years which now have evanesced in memory like a dream at dawn. When I became fifteen I returned to my own Valverde de Lucerna. By now everything    revolved around Don Manuel: Don Manuel, the lake, and the mountain. I arrived home eager to know him, to place myself under his protection, hoping he would set me on my path in life.

It was rumored that he had entered the seminary to become a priest so that he might look after the sons of a sister recently widowed and provide for them in place of their father; that in the seminary his keen mind and his talents had distinguished him, and that he had subsequently turned down opportunities for a brilliant career in the church because he wanted to remain a part of his Valverde de Lucerna, of his remote village which lay like a brooch between the lake and the mountain reflected in it.

How did he love his people! His life consisted in

rescuing wrecked marriages, in forcing unruly sons to submit to their parents, or reconciling parents to their sons; but above all: consoling the embittered and the weary in spirit, while helping everyone to die well.

I recall, among other incidents, the time when the unfortunate daughter of old aunt Rabona returned to our town, having been in the city where she her virtue. Now she returned unmarried and castoff, and bringing a little son. Don Manuel did not rest until he had persuaded an old sweetheart —Perote by name— not only to marry the poor girl, but also to legitimize the little creature with his own name. Don Manuel told Perote:

"Come now, give this poor lost child a father, for he hasn't got one except in heaven."

"But, Don Manuel, it's not my fault...!"

"Who knows, my son, who knows...! And besides, it's not a question of guilt."

And today, poor Perote, inspired on that occasion to saintliness by Don Manuel, and now a paralytic and invalid, has for staff and consolation of his life the son he accepted as his own when the boy was not his at all.

On Midsummer's Night, the shortest night of the year, it

was a local custom here (and still is) for all the old harpies, and a few old men, who thought they were possessed or bewitched (hysterics they were, for the most part, or in some cases epileptics) to flock to the lake.

There Don Manuel endeavored to fulfill the same function as the lake: to serve as a pool of healing, to treat his charges and even, if possible, to cure them. And such was the effect of his presence, of his gaze, and above all of his voice—the miracle of his voice!—and the infinitely sweet authority of his words, that he actually did achieve some notable cures. By all that, his fame increased, drawing all the sick of the environs to our lake and to our priest. And yet once when a mother came to ask for a miracle on behalf of her son, he answered her with a sad smile:

"Ah, but I don't have my bishop's permission to perform miracles."

Seeing that all the villagers kept themselves clean, was of particular interest to him. If he saw someone with a torn garment he would send him to the church: "Go and see the sacristan, and let him mend that tear." The sacristan was a tailor, and when, on the first day of the year, everyone went to congratulate him on his saint's day—his

7

holy patron was Our Lord Jesus Himself—it was by Don Manuel's wish that everyone appeared in a new shirt, and those that lacked one received the gift of a new one from Don Manuel himself.

He treated everyone with the greatest kindness; if he favored anyone, it was the most unfortunate, and especially those who rebelled. There was a congenital idiot in the village, the fool Blasillo, and it was toward him that Don Manuel chose to show the greatest love and care; as a result he succeeded in miraculously teaching him things which had appeared beyond the idiot's grasp. The fact was that the embers of understanding feebly glowing in the idiot were kindled whenever, like a pitiable monkey, he imitated his Don Manuel.

The marvel of Don Manuel was his voice; a divine voice which brought one close to weeping. Whenever he said a Solemn High Mass and intoned the prelude, a tremor ran through the congregation and all within sound of his voice were moved to the depths of their being. The sound of his chanting, overflowing the church, went on to float over the lake and settle at the foot of the mountain. And when on Good Friday he intoned "My God, my God, my God, why hast Thou forsaken me?" a profound shudder swept through the multitude, like the lash of a northeaster across the waters of the lake. It was as if our people heard the Lord Jesus Christ himself, as if the voice sprang from the ancient crucifix, at the foot of which generations of mothers had offered up their sorrows.

And it happened that on one occasion his mother heard him and was unable to contain herself, and cried out to him right in the church, "My son!," calling her child. And the entire congregation was visibly affected. It was as if the mother's cry had issued from the half-open lips of the Mater Dolorosa—her heart transfixed by seven swords—which stood in one of the chapels of the nave. Afterwards, the fool Blasillo went about piteously repeating, as if he were an echo, "My God, my God, my God, why hast Thou forsaken me?" with such effect that everyone who heard him was moved to tears, to the great satisfaction of the fool, who prided himself on this triumph of imitation.

The priest's effect on people was such that no one ever dared to tell him a lie, and everyone confessed himself to him without need of a confessional. So true was this that on one occasion, when a heinous crime had been committed in a neighboring village, the judge—a dull fellow who badly misunderstood Don Manuel— called on the priest and said:

"Let's see, Don Manuel, if you can get this bandit to admit the truth."

"So that afterwards you may punish him?" asked the saintly man. "No, Judge, no; I will not extract from any man a truth which would kill him. That is a matter between him and his God.... Human justice is none of my affair. Judge not that ye be not judged, said our Lord."

"But the fact is, Father, that I, a judge ..."

"I understand. You, Judge, must render unto Caesar that which is Caesar's, while I shall render unto God that which is God's."

And, as Don Manuel departed, he gazed at the suspected criminal and said:

"Make sure that only God forgives you, for that is all that matters."

Everyone went to Mass in the village, even if it were only to hear him and see him at the altar, where he appeared to be transfigured, his countenance lit from within. He introduced one holy practice to the popular cult; it consisted in getting the whole town inside the church, men and women, ancients and youths, some thousand persons; there we recited the Creed, in unison, so that it sounded like a single voice: "I believe in God, the Almighty Father, Creator of heaven and earth ..." and all the rest. It was not a chorus, but a single voice, a simple united voice, all the voices based on one on which they formed a kind of mountain, whose peak, lost at times in the clouds, was Don Manuel. As we reached the section "I believe in the resurrection of the flesh and life everlasting," the voice of Don Manuel was submerged, drowned in the voice of the populace as in a lake.

In truth, he was silent.

And I could hear the bells of that city which is said around here to be at the bottom of the lake—bells which are also said to be audible on Midsummer's Night—the bells of the city which is submerged in the spiritual lake of our populace. I was hearing the voice of our dead, resurrected in us by the communion of saints. Later, when I had learned the secret of our saint, I understood that it was as if a caravan crossing the desert lost its leader as they approached the goal of their journey, whereupon his people lifted him on their shoulders to bring his lifeless body into the Promised Land.

When it came to dying, most of the villagers refused to die unless they were holding on to Don Manuel's hand, as if to an anchor chain.

In his sermons he never lashed against unbelievers, Masons, liberals or heretics. What for?
There were none in the village! Nor did it occur to him to speak against the wickedness of the press. On the other hand, one of his most frequent themes was gossip, against which he lashed out.

"Envy" he liked to repeat, "envy is nurtured by those who prefer to think they are envied, and most persecutions are the result of a persecution complex rather than of an impulse to persecute."

"But Don Manuel, just listen to what that fellow was trying to tell me ..."

"We should concern ourselves less with what people are trying to tell us than with what they tell us without trying..."

His life was active rather than contemplative,

constantly fleeing from idleness, even from leisure.

Whenever he heard someone say that idleness was the mother of all the vices, he added: "And also of the greatest vice of them all, which is to think idly." Once I asked him what he meant and he answered: "Thinking idly is thinking as a substitute for doing, or thinking too much about what is already done instead of about what must be done. What's done is done and over with, and one must go on to something else, because nothing is worse than remorse without possible relief."

Action! Action! Even in those early days I had already begun to realize that Don Manuel fled from being left to think in solitude, and I guessed that some obsession haunted him.

That is why he was always occupied; sometimes even occupied in searching for occupations. He wrote very little on his own, so that he scarcely left us anything in writing, even notes; on the other hand, he acted as scrivener for everyone else, especially mothers, for whom he composed letters to their absent sons.

He also worked with his hands, pitching in to help with some of the village tasks. At threshing time he joined in the threshing floor to flair and winnow, while teaching and entertaining the workers by turn. Sometimes he took the place of a worker who had fallen sick. One day in the dead of winter he came upon a child, shivering with the bitter cold. The child's father had sent him into the woods to bring back a strayed calf.

"Listen," he said to the child, "you go home and get warm, and tell your father that I am bringing back the calf." On the way back with the animal he ran into the father, who had come out to meet him, thoroughly ashamed of himself.

In winter he chopped wood for the poor. When a certain magnificent walnut tree died— "that matriarchal walnut," he called it, a tree under whose shade he had played as a boy and whose fruit he had eaten for so many years—he asked for the trunk, carrying it to his house. After he had cut six planks from it, which he put away at the foot of his bed, he made firewood of the rest to warm the poor. He also was in the habit of making handballs for the boys and a goodly number of toys for the younger children.

Often he used to accompany the doctor on his rounds,

adding his presence and prestige to the doctor's prescriptions. Most of all he was interested in maternity cases and the care of children; it was his opinion that the old wives' sayings "from the cradle to heaven" and the other one about "little angels belong in heaven" were short of blasphemy. The death of a child moved him deeply.

"A child stillborn," I once heard him say, "or one who dies soon after birth, is the most terrible of mysteries to me. It's as if it were a suicide. Or as if the child were crucified."

Once, when a man had taken his own life and the father of the suicide, an outsider, asked Don Manuel if his son could be buried in consecrated ground, the priest answered:

"Yes, of course! At the last moment, in the very last throes, he must surely have repented. There is no doubt of it whatsoever in my mind."

Once in a while he would visit the local school to help the teacher, to teach alongside him—and not only the catechism. The simple truth was that he fled relentlessly from idleness and from solitude. He went so far in this desire of his to mingle with the villagers, especially the youth and the children, that he even attended the village dances. And more than once he played the drum to keep time for the young men and women dancing; this kind of activity, which in another priest would have seemed like a grotesque mockery of his calling, in him somehow took on the appearance of a holy and religious exercise.

When the Angelus would ring out, he would put down the drum and sticks, take off his hat (all the others doing the same) and pray: "The angel of the Lord declared unto Mary: Hail Mary..." And afterwards: "Now, let us rest until tomorrow."

"First of all" he would say, "the village must be happy; everyone must be happy to be alive. To be satisfied with life is of first importance. No one should want to die until it is God's will."

"I want to die now," a recently widowed woman once told him, "I want to be with my husband ..."

"And why now?" he asked. "Stay here and pray God for his soul."

One of his well-loved sayings he made at a wedding: "Ah, if I could only change all the water in our lake into wine, into a dear little wine which, no matter how much of it one drank, would always make one joyful without intoxicating... or, if intoxicating, would make one joyfully drunk."

Once a band of poor acrobats came through the village, and the leader—who arrived on the scene with a gravely ill and pregnant wife and three sons to help him—played the clown. While he was in the village square making all the children, and even some of the adults, laugh with glee, his wife suddenly fell desperately ill and had to leave; she went off accompanied by a look of anguish from the clown and a howl of laughter from the children. Don Manuel hurried after, and, a little later, in a corner of the inn's stable, he helped her give up her soul in a state of grace. When the performance was over and the villagers and the clown learned of the tragedy, they came to the inn, and there the poor bereaved clown, in a voice choked with tears, told Don Manuel, as he took his hand and kissed it: "They are quite right, Father, when they say you are a saint." Don Manuel took the clown's hand in his and replied before everyone:

"You are the saint—good clown! I watched you at your work and understood that you do it not only to provide bread for your children, but also to give joy to the children of others. And I tell you now that your wife, the mother of your children, whom I sent to God while you worked to give joy, is at rest in the Lord, and that you will join her there, and that the angels, whom you will make laugh with happiness in heaven, will reward you with their laughter."

And everyone present wept, children and elders alike, as much from sorrow as from a mysterious joy in which all sorrow was drowned.

Later, recalling that solemn hour, I came to realize that the serene joy of Don Manuel was merely a temporal, earthly form of an infinite and eternal sadness, something which the priest hid from the eyes and ears of the world with heroic saintliness.

His constant activity, his unending intervention in the tasks and diversions of everyone, had the appearance, in short, of a flight from himself, of a flight from solitude. He confirmed this suspicion: "I have a fear of solitude," he would say. And still, from time to time he would go off by himself, along the shores of the lake, to the ruins of the abbey where the souls of pious Cistercians seem still to repose, although history has long since buried them in oblivion. There, the cell of the so-called Father-Captain can still be found, and it is said that the drops of blood spattered on the walls as he flagellated himself can still be seen.

What thoughts occupied our Don Manuel as he walked there?

I remember a conversation we held once in which I asked him, as he was speaking of the abbey, why it had never occurred to him to enter a monastery, and he answered me:

"It is not at all because of the fact that my sister is a widow and I have her children and herself to support—for God looks after the poor—but rather because I simply was not born to be a hermit, an anchorite; the solitude would crush my soul; and, as far as a monastery is concerned, my monastery is Valverde de Lucerna.

"I was not meant to live alone, or die alone.

"I was meant to live for my village, and die for it too. How should I save my soul if I were not to save the soul of my village as well?"

"But there have been saints who were hermits, solitaries

19

..." I said.

"Yes, the Lord gave them the grace of solitude which He has denied me, and I must resign myself. I must not throw away my village to win my soul. God made me that way. I would not be able to resist the temptations of the desert. I would not be able, alone, to carry the cross of birth..."

I have brought up all these recollections, from which my faith was fed, in order to portray our Don Manuel as he was when I, a young girl of sixteen, returned from the convent of Renada to our "monastery of Valverde de Lucerna," once more to kneel at the feet of our "abbot."

"Well, here is the daughter of Simona," he said as soon as he saw me, "made into a young woman, and knowing French, and how to play the piano, and embroider, and heaven knows what else besides! Now you must get ready to give us a family. And your brother Lazarus; when does he return? Is he still in the New World?"

"Yes, Father, he is still in the New World."

"The New World! And we in the Old. Well then, when you write him, tell him for me, on behalf of the parish priest, that I should like to know when he is returning from the New World to the Old, to bring us the latest from over there. And tell him that he will find the lake and the mountain as he left them."

When I first went to him for confession, I became so confused that I could not speak a word. I recited the "Forgive me, Father, for I have sinned," in a stammer, almost a sob. And he, observing this, said:

"Good heavens, my dear, what are you afraid of, or of whom are you afraid? Certainly you're not trembling now under the weight of your sins, nor in fear of God. No, you're trembling because of me, isn't that so?"

Right then I burst into tears.

"What have they been telling you about me? What fairy tales? Was it your mother, perhaps? Come, come, please be calm; you must imagine you are talking to your brother ..."

Plucking up courage I began to tell him of my anxieties, doubts, and sorrows.

"Heavens! Where did you read all this—Miss Intellectual. All this is literary nonsense. Don't succumb to everything you read just yet, not even to Saint Theresa. If you need to amuse yourself, read the *Bertoldo,* as your father before you did."

Deeply consoled I came away from my first confession

to that holy man. The initial fear— simple fright more than respect—with which I had approached him, turned into a profound pity. I was at that time a very young woman, almost a girl still; and yet, I was beginning to be a woman, in my innermost being I felt the juice and stirrings of maternity. And when I found myself in the confessional at the side of the saintly priest, I sensed a kind of unspoken confession on his part in the soft murmur of his voice. And I remembered how when he had intoned in the church the words of Jesus Christ: "My God, my God, why hast Thou forsaken me?" his own mother had cried out in the congregation: "My son!"; and I could hear the cry that had held the silence of the temple. And I went to him again for confession—and to comfort him.

Another time in the confessional I told him of a doubt which assailed me, and he responded:

"As to that, you know what the catechism says. Don't question me about it, for I am ignorant; in Holy Mother Church there are learned doctors of theology who will know how to answer you."

"But you are the learned doctor here."

"Me? A learned doctor? Not even in thought! I, my

little doctress, am only a poor country priest. And those questions,... do you know who whispers them into your ear? Well.. . the Devil does!"

Then, making bold, I asked him point-blank:

"And suppose he were to whisper these questions to you?"

"Who? To me? The Devil? No, we don't even know each other, my daughter, we haven't met at all."

"But if he did whisper them? ..."

"I wouldn't pay any attention. And enough of that; let's get on, for there are some people, really sick people, waiting for me."

I went away thinking, I don't know why, that our Don Manuel, so famous for curing the bedeviled, didn't really even believe in the Devil. As I started home, I ran into the fool Blasillo, who had probably been hovering around outside; as soon as he saw me, and by way of treating me to a display of his virtuosity, he began the business of repeating—and in what a manner!—'My God, my God, why hast Thou forsaken me?" I arrived home so utterly saddened that I locked myself in my room to cry, until finally my mother arrived.

"With all these confessions, Angelita, you will end by going off to a nunnery."

"Don't worry, Mother," I answered her. "I have plenty to do here, in the village, and it will be my only convent."

"Until you marry."

"I don't intend to," I rejoined.

The next time I saw Don Manuel I asked him, looking straight into his eyes:

"Is there really a Hell, Don Manuel?"

Without altering his expression, he answered:

"For you, my daughter—no."

"For others, then?"

"Does it matter to you, if you are not to go there?"

"It matters for the others, in any case. Is there a Hell?"

"Believe in Heaven, the Heaven we can see. Look at it there"—and he pointed to the heavens above the mountain, and then down into the lake, to the reflection.

"But we are supposed to believe in Hell as well as in Heaven," I said.

"That's true. We must believe everything believed and taught by our Holy Mother Church, Catholic, Apostolic, and Roman. And now, that will do!"

I thought I read a deep unknown sadness in his eyes, eyes which were as blue as the waters of the lake.

Those years passed as if in a dream. Within me, a reflected image of Don Manuel was unconsciously taking form. He was an ordinary enough man in many ways, of such daily use as the daily bread we asked for in our Paternoster. I helped him whenever I could with his tasks, visiting the sick, his sick, the girls at school, and helping, too, with the church linen and the vestments. I served in the role, as he said, of his deaconess. Once I was invited to the city for a few days by a school friend, but I had to hurry home, for the city stifled me—something was missing. I was thirsty for a sight of the waters of the lake, hungry for a sight of the peaks of the mountain; and even more, I missed my Don Manuel, as if his absence called to me, as if he were endangered by my being so far away, as if he were in need of me.

I began to feel a kind of maternal affection for my spiritual father; I longed to help him bear the cross of birth.

My twenty-fourth birthday was approaching when my brother Lazarus came back from America with the small fortune he had saved up.

He came back to Valverde de Lucerna with the intention of taking me and my mother to live in a city, perhaps even Madrid.

"In the country," he said, "in these villages, a person becomes dull, brutalized, and spiritually poor." And he added: "Civilization is the very opposite of everything countrified. The idiocy of village life! No, that's not for us; I didn't have you sent away to school so that later you might spoil here, among these ignorant peasants."

I said nothing, though I was disposed to resist emigration. But our mother, already past sixty, took a firm stand from the start: "To change pastures at my age?" she demanded at once. A little later she made it quite clear that she could not live out of sight of her lake, her mountain, and, above all, of her Don Manuel.

"The two of you are like those cats that get attached to houses," my brother muttered.

When he realized the complete sway exercised over the entire village—especially over my mother and myself—by the saintly priest, my brother began to resent him. He saw in this situation an example of the obscurantist theocracy which, according to him, smothered Spain. And he commenced to spout the old anti-clerical commonplaces, to which he added anti-religious and "progressive" propaganda brought back from the New World.

"In the Spain of sloth and flabby useless men, the priests manipulate the women, and the women manipulate the men. Not to mention the idiocy of the country, and this feudal backwater !"

"Feudal," to him, meant something frightful. "Feudal" and "medieval" were the epithets he employed to totally condemn something.

The failure of his diatribes to move us and their total lack of effect upon the village—where they were listened to with respectful indifference—disconcerted him no end. "The man does not exist who could move these clods." But, he soon began to understand—for he was an intelligent man, and therefore a good one—the kind of influence exercised over the village by Don Manuel, and he came to appreciate the effect of the priest's work in the village.

"This priest is unlike the others," he announced. "He

is, in fact, a saint."

"How do you know what the others are like," I asked. To which he answered:

"I can imagine."

In any case, he never set foot inside the church, nor did he miss a chance to display his incredulity—though he always exempted Don Manuel from his scorning accusations. In the village, an unconscious expectancy began to pent up, an sort of anticipation of a duel between my brother Lazarus and Don Manuel—in short, it was expected that Don Manuel would convert my brother.

No one doubted but that in the end the priest would bring him into the fold.

On his side, Lazarus was eager (he told me so himself, later) to go and hear Don Manuel, to see and hear him in the church, to get to know him and to talk with him, so that he might learn the secret of his spiritual hold over our souls. And he let himself be coaxed to this end, so that finally—"out of curiosity," as he said—he went to hear the preacher.

"Now, this is something else again," he told me as soon as he came from hearing Don Manuel for the first time. "He's not like the others; still, he doesn't fool me; he's far too intelligent to believe everything he must teach."

"You mean you think he's a hypocrite?"

"A hypocrite... no! But he has a job by which he must live."

As for me, my brother undertook to see that I read the books he brought me, and others which he urged me to buy.

"So your brother Lazarus wants you to read," Don Manuel asked. "Well, read, my daughter, read and make him happy by doing so. I know you will read only worthy books. Read even if only novels; they are as good as the books which deal with so-called 'reality.' You are better off reading than concerning yourself with village gossip and old wives' tales. Above all, though, you will do well to read devotional books which will bring you contentment in life, a quiet, gentle contentment, and peace."

And he, did he enjoy such contentment?

About this time our mother fell mortally sick and died. In her last days her one wish was that Don Manuel should convert Lazarus, whom she expected to see again in heaven, in some little corner among the stars from where they could see the lake and the mountain of Valverde de Lucerna. She felt she was going there now, to see God.

"You are not going anywhere," Don Manuel would tell her; "you are staying right here. Your body will remain here, in this land, and your soul also, in this house, watching and listening to your children though they do not see or hear you."

"But, Father," she said, "I am going to see God."

"God, my daughter, is all around us, and you will see Him from here, right from here. And all of us in Him, and He in all of us."

"God bless you," I whispered to him.

"The peace in which your mother dies will be her eternal life," he told me.

And, turning to my brother Lazarus: "Her heaven is to go on seeing you, and it is at this moment that she must be saved. Tell her you will pray for her."

"But—"

"But what? ... Tell her you will pray for her, to whom you owe your life. And I know that once you promise her, you *will* pray, and I know that once you pray ..."

My brother, his eyes filled with tears, drew near our dying mother and gave her his solemn promise to pray for her.

"And I, in heaven, will pray for you, for all of you," my mother responded. And then, kissing the crucifix and fixing her eyes on Don Manuel, she gave up her soul to God.

"Into Thy hands I commend my spirit," prayed the priest.

My brother and I stayed on in the house—alone. What had happened at the time of my mother's death had formed a bond between Lazarus and Don Manuel. The latter seemed even to neglect some of his charges, his patients and his other needy to look after my brother. In the afternoons, they would go for a stroll together, walking along the lake or toward the ruins, overgrown with ivy, of the old Cistercian abbey.

"He's an extraordinary man," Lazarus told me. "You know the story they tell of how there is a city at the bottom of the lake, submerged beneath the water, and that on Midsummer's Night at midnight the sound of its church bells can be heard ..."

31

"Yes, a city 'feudal and medieval'..."

"And I believe," he went on, "that at the bottom of Don Manuel's soul there is a city, submerged and inundated, and that sometimes the sound of its bells can be heard ..."

"Yes ... And this city submerged in Don Manuel's soul, and perhaps—why not?—in yours as well, is certainly the cemetery of the souls of our ancestors, the ancestors of our Valverde de Lucerna ... 'feudal and medieval.'"

In the end, my brother began going to Mass regularly to hear Don Manuel. When it became known that he was prepared to comply with his annual duty of receiving Communion, that he would receive when the others received, an intimate joy ran through the town, which felt that by this act he was restored to his people. The rejoicing was of such nature, moreover, so openhanded and honest, that Lazarus never did feel that he had been "vanquished" or "overcome."

The day of his Communion —before and with the entire village— arrived.

When it came time for my brother's turn, I saw Don Manuel—white as January snow on the mountain, and moving like the surface of the lake when it is stirred by the northeast wind—come up to him with the holy wafer in his hand, which trembled violently as it reached out to Lazarus's mouth. At that moment the priest had an instant of faintness and the wafer dropped to the ground. My brother himself recovered it and placed it in his mouth. The people saw the tears on Don Manuel's face, and everyone wept, saying: "What great love he bears!" And then, because it was dawn, a cock crowed.

On returning home I locked myself in with my brother; alone with him I put my arms around his neck and kissed him.

"Lazarus, Lazarus, what joy you have given us all today; the entire village, the living and the dead, and especially our mother. Did you see how Don Manuel wept for joy? What joy you have given us all!"

"I did what I did just for that reason," he answered me.

"For what? To give us pleasure? Surely you did it for your own sake, first of all; because of your conversion."

And then Lazarus, my brother, grown as pale and tremulous as Don Manuel when he was giving Communion, bade me sit down, in the very chair where

33

our mother used to sit. He took a deep breath, and, in the intimate tone of a familiar and domestic confession, he told me:

"Angelita, the time has come when I must tell you the truth, the absolute truth, and I shall tell you because I must, because I cannot, I ought not, hide it from you, and because, sooner or later, you are bound to intuit it anyway, if only halfway—which would be worse."

With a serene, tranquil, and subdued voice, he recounted a tale that drowned me in a lake of sorrow. He told how Don Manuel had appealed to him, particularly during the walks to the ruins of the old Cistercian abbey, to set a good example, to avoid scandalizing the townspeople, to take part in the religious life of the community, to feign belief even if he did not feel any, to conceal his own ideas—all this without attempting in any way to catechize him, to instruct him in religion, or to effect a true conversion.

"But is it possible?" I asked in consternation.

"Possible and true. When I said to him: 'Is this you, the priest, who suggests I dissimulate?' he replied, hesitatingly: 'Dissimulate? Not at all! That is not dissimulation. "Dip your fingers in holy water, and you will end by believing," as someone said, And I, gazing into his eyes, asked him: And you, celebrating the Mass, have you ended by believing?' He looked away and stared out at the lake, until his eyes filled with tears. And it was in this way that I came to understand his secret."

"Lazarus!" I cried out, incapable of another word.

At that moment the fool Blasillo came along our street, crying out his: "My God, my God, why hast Thou forsaken me?" And Lazarus shuddered, as if he had heard the voice of Don Manuel, or of Christ.

"In that instant," my brother at length continued, "that I really understood his motives and his saintliness; for a saint he is, Sister, a true saint. In trying to convert me to his holy cause—for it is a holy cause, a most holy cause—he was not trying to score a triumph, but rather was doing it to protect the peace, the happiness, the illusions, perhaps, of his parishioners.

"I understood that if he thus deceives them—if it *is* deceit—it is not for his own advantage. I submitted to his logic,—and that was my conversion.

"I shall never forget the day on which I said to him: 'But, Don Manuel, the truth, the truth, above all!'; and he, all shook up, whispered in my ear—though we were all alone in the middle of the countryside—The truth? The truth, Lazarus, is perhaps something so unbearable, so terrible, something so deadly, that simple people could not live with it!'

"'And why do you show me a glimpse of it now, here, as if we were in the confessional?' I asked. And he said: 'Because if I did not, I would be so tormented by it, so tormented, that I would finally shout it in the middle of the plaza, which I must never, never, never do ... I am put here to give life to the souls of my charges, to make them happy, to make them dream they are immortal—and not to destroy them. The important thing is that they live sanely, in harmony with each other,—and with the truth, with my truth, they could not live at all. Let them live. That is what the Church does, it lets them live. As for true religion, all religions are true as long as they give spiritual life to the people who profess them, as long as they console them for having been born only to die. And for people the truest religion is their own, the religion that made them . . . And mine? Mine consists in consoling myself by consoling others, even though the consolation I give them is not ever mine.' I shall never forget his words."

"But then this Communion of yours has been a sacrilege," I dared interrupt, regretting my words as soon as I said them.

"Sacrilege? What about the priest who gave it to me? And his Masses?"

"What martyrdom!" I exclaimed.

"And now," said my brother, "there is one more person to console the people."

"To deceive them, you mean?" I said.

"Not at all," he replied, "but rather to confirm them in their faith."

"And they, the people, do they really believe, do you think?"

"About that, I know nothing!... They probably believe without trying, from force of habit, and tradition. What matters is not to stir them up. To let them live from their thin sentiments, without acquiring the torments of luxury. Blessed are the poor in spirit!"

"That then is the sentiment you have learned from Don Manuel.... And tell me, do you feel you have carried out your promise to our mother on her deathbed, when you promised to pray for her?"

"Do you think I *could* fail her? What do you take me for, sister? Do you think I would go back on my word, my solemn promise made at the hour of death to a mother?"

"I don't know.... You might have wanted to deceive her so she could die in peace."

"The fact is, though, that if I had not lived up to my promise, I would be totally miserable."

"And ..."

"I carried out my promise and I have not neglected for a single day to pray for her."

"Only for her?"

"Well, now, for whom else?"

"For yourself! And now, for Don Manuel."

We parted and went to our separate rooms. I to weep through the night, praying for the conversion of my brother and of Don Manuel. And Lazarus, to what purpose, I know not.

From that day on I was fearful of finding myself alone with Don Manuel, whom I continued to aid in his pious works. And he seemed to sense my inner state and to guess at its cause. When at last I came to him in the confessional's penitential tribunal (who was the judge, and who the offender?) the two of us, he and I, bowed our heads in silence and began to cry. Finally, Don Manuel broke the terrible silence, with a voice which seemed to come from the tomb:

"Angelita, you have the same faith you had when you were ten, don't you? You believe, don't you?"

"I believe, Father."

"Then go on believing. And if doubts come to torment you, suppress them utterly, even to yourself. The main thing is to live ..."

I summoned up courage, and dared to ask, trembling:

"But, Father, do you believe?"

For a brief moment he hesitated, and then, mastering himself, he said:

"I believe!"

"In what, Father, in what? Do you believe in the afterlife? Do you believe that in dying we do not die in every way, completely? Do you believe that we will see each other again, that we will love each other in a world to come? Do you believe in another life?"

39

The poor saint was sobbing.

"My child, let it be—let it be!"

Now, as I write this memoir, I ask myself: Why didn't he deceive me? Why did he not deceive me as he deceived the others? Why did he afflict himself? Why could he not deceive himself, or why could he not deceive me? And I want to believe that he was afflicted because he could not deceive himself into deceiving me.

"And now," he said, "pray for me, for your brother, and for yourself—for all of us. We must go on living. And giving life."

And, after a pause:

"Angelita, why don't you marry?"

"You know why I do not."

"No, no; you must marry. Lazarus and I will find you a suitor. For it would be good for you to marry, and rid yourself of these obsessions."

"Obsessions, Don Manuel?"

"I know well enough what I am saying. You should not torment yourself for the sake of others, for each of us has more than enough to do answering for himself."

"That it should be you, Don Manuel, who says this!

That you should advise me to marry and answer for myself alone and not suffer over others! That it should be you!"

"Yes, you are right, Angelita. I am no longer sure of what I say. I am no longer sure of what I say since I began to confess to you. Only, one must go on living. Yes! One must live!"

And when I rose to leave the church, he asked me:

"Now, Angelita, in the name of the people, do you absolve me?"

I felt pierced by a mysterious and priestly prompting and said:

"In the name of the Father, the Son and the Holy Ghost, I absolve you, Father."

We left the church, and as I went out I felt the quickening of maternity within me.

My brother, now totally devoted to the work of Don Manuel, becoming his closest and most zealous collaborator and companion. They were bound together, moreover, by their common secret. Lazarus accompanied the priest on his visits to the sick, and to schools, placing his resources at the disposition of the saintly man. A little

41

more zeal and he would have learned to help celebrate Mass. All the while he was sounding deeper in the unfathomable soul of the priest.

"What manliness!" he exclaimed to me once. "Yesterday, as we walked along the lake he said: 'There lies my direst temptation.' When I interrogated him with my eyes, he went on: 'My poor father, who was close to ninety when he died, was tormented all his life, as he confessed to me himself, by a temptation to suicide, by an instinct to self-destruction which had come to him from a time before memory— from birth, from his *nation,* as he said—and was forced to fight against it always. And this fight grew to be his life. So as not to succumb to this temptation he was forced to take precautions, to guard his life. He told me of terrible episodes. His urge was a form of madness,— and I have inherited it. How that water beckons me in its deep quiet!... an apparent quietude reflecting the sky like a mirror—and beneath it the hidden current! My life, Lazarus, is a kind of continual suicide, or a struggle against suicide, which is the same thing... Just so long as our people go on living!' And then he added: 'Here the river eddies to form a lake, so that later, flowing down the plateau, it may form into cascades, waterfalls, and torrents, hurling itself through gorges and chasms. So does life eddy in the village; and the temptation to suicide is the greater beside the still waters which at night reflect the stars, than it is beside the crashing falls which drive one back in fear. Listen, Lazarus, I have helped poor villagers to die well, ignorant, illiterate villagers, who had scarcely ever been out of their village, and I have learned from their own lips, or divined it when they were silent, the real cause of their sickness unto death, and there at the head of their deathbed I have been able to see into the black abyss of their life-weariness. Weariness a thousand times worse than hunger! For our part, Lazarus, let us go on with our kind of suicide of working for the people, and let them dream their life as the lake dreams the heavens.

"Another time," said my brother, "as we were coming back, we spied a country girl, a goatherd, standing erect on a height of the mountain slope overlooking the lake and she was singing in a voice fresher than its waters. Don Manuel took hold of me, and pointing to her said: 'Look, it's as though time has stopped, as though this country girl has always been there just as she is, singing in the way she is, and as though she will always be there, as she was before my consciousness began, as she will be when it is past. That girl is a part of nature—not of history—along with the rocks, the clouds, the trees, and the waters. He has such a subtle feeling for nature, he infuses it with spirit.

"I shall not forget the day when snow was falling and he asked me: 'Have you ever seen a greater mystery, Lazarus, than the snow falling, and dying, in the lake, while a hood is laid upon the mountain?' "

Don Manuel had to moderate and temper my brother's zeal and his neophyte's rawness. As soon as he heard that Lazarus was going about inveighing against some of the popular superstitions he told him forcefully:

"Leave them alone! It's difficult enough making them understand where orthodox belief leaves off and where superstition begins. It's hard enough, especially for us. Leave them alone, then, as long as they get some comfort. ... It's better for them to believe everything, even things that contradict one another, than to believe nothing. The idea that someone who believes too much ends by not

44

believing in anything is a Protestant notion. Let us not protest! Protestation destroys contentment and peace."

My brother told me, too, about one moonlit night when they were returning to town along the lake (whose surface a mountain breeze was stirring, so that the moonbeams topped the whitecaps), Don Manuel turned to him and said:

"Look, the water is reciting the litany and saying: *ianua caeli, ora pro nobis;* gate of heaven, pray for us."

Two evanescent tears fell from his eye lashes to the grass, where the light of the full moon shone upon them like dew.

As time went hurrying by, my brother and I began to notice that Don Manuel's spirits were failing, that he could no longer control completely the deep rooted sadness which consumed him; perhaps some treacherous illness was undermining his body and soul. In an effort to rouse his interest, Lazarus spoke to him of the good effect the organization of a type of Catholic agrarian syndicate would have.

"A syndicate?" Don Manuel repeated sadly. "A syndicate? And what is that? The Church is the only syndicate I know. And you have certainly heard 'My kingdom is not of this world. Our kingdom, Lazarus, is not of this world ...'"

"And of the other?"

Don Manuel bowed his head:

"The other is here. Two kingdoms exist in this world. Or rather, the other world. . . . Ah, I don't really know what I'm saying. But as for the syndicate, that's a vestige from your days of 'progressivism.' No, Lazarus, no; religion does not exist to resolve the economic or political conflicts of this world, which God handed over to men for their disputes. Let men think and act as they will, let them console themselves for having been born, let them live as happily as possible in the illusion that all this has a purpose. I don't propose to advise the poor to submit to the rich, nor to suggest to the rich that they subordinate themselves to the poor; but rather to preach resignation in everyone, and charity toward everyone. For even the rich man must resign himself—to his riches, and to life. And the poor man must show charity—even to the rich.

"The Social Question? Ignore it, for it is none of our business. So, a new society is on the way, in which there will be neither rich nor poor, in which wealth will be justly divided, in which everything will belong to everyone—and so, what then? Won't this general well-being and comfort lead to even greater tedium and weariness of life? I know well enough that one of those leaders of what they call the Social Revolution has already said that religion is the opium of the people. Opium ... Opium . . . Yes, opium it is. We should give *them* opium, and help them sleep, and dream. I, myself, with my mad activity, give myself opium. And still I don't manage to sleep well, let alone dream well. . . . What a horrible nightmare! ... I, too, can say, with the Divine Master: 'My soul is weary unto death.' No, Lazarus, no; no syndicates for us. If *they* organize them, well and good—they would be distracting themselves in that way. Let them play at syndicates, if that makes them happy"

The entire village began to realize that Don Manuel's spirit was weakening, that his strength was waning. His very voice—that miracle of a voice—acquired a kind of quaking. Tears came into his eyes for any reason whatever—or for no reason. Whenever he spoke to people about the other world, about the other life, he was compelled to pause at frequent intervals, and he would close his eyes. "It is a vision," people would say, "he has a vision of what lies ahead." At such moments the fool Blasillo was the first to break into tears, weeping copiously these days, crying now more than he laughed, and even his laughter had the sound of tears.

The last Easter Week which Don Manuel was to celebrate among us, in this world, in this village of ours, arrived, and the village sensed the impending tragedy—the end.

And how the words did strike home when for the last time Don Manuel cried out before us: "My God, my God, why hast Thou forsaken me?"! And when he repeated the words of the Lord to the Good Thief ('All thieves are good,' Don Manuel used to tell us): "Tomorrow shalt thou be with me in Paradise." ... And then, at the last general Communion which our saint was to give, When he came to my brother to give him the Host—his hand steady this time—, just after the liturgical "... *in vitam aeternam*" he bent down and whispered to him: "There is no other life but this, no life more eternal... let them dream it eternal...

let it be eternal for a few years . . ."

And when he came to me he said: "Pray, my child, pray for us all." And then, something so extraordinary happened that I carry it now in my heart as the greatest of mysteries: he bent over and said, in a voice which seemed to belong to the other world: "... and pray, too, for our Lord Jesus Christ."

I stood up, growing weak as I did so, like a somnambulist. Everything around me seemed dream-like. And I thought: "Am I to pray, too, for the lake and the mountain?" And next: "Am I bewitched, then?" Home at last, I took up the crucifix my mother had held in her hands when she had given up her soul to God, and, gazing at it through my tears and recalling the "My God, my God, why hast Thou forsaken me?" of our two Christs, the one of this earth and the other of this village, I prayed: "Thy will be done on earth as it is in heaven," and then, "And lead us not into temptation. Amen." After this I turned to the statue of the Mater Dolorosa—her heart transfixed by seven swords—which had been my poor mother's most sorrowful comfort, and I prayed again: "Holy Mary, Mother of God, pray for us sinners, now and in the hour of our death. Amen."

Scarcely had I finished the prayer, when I asked myself: "Sinners? Sinners are we? And what is our sin, what is it?" And all day I brooded over the question.

The next day I presented myself before Don Manuel—Don Manuel now in the full sunset of his magnificent religiosity—and I said to him:

"Do you remember, my Father, years ago when I asked you a certain question you answered: 'That question you must not ask me; for I am ignorant; there are learned doctors of the Holy Mother Church who will know how to answer you'?"

"Do I remember?... Of course. And I remember I told you those were questions put to you by the Devil."

"Well, then, Father, I have come again, bedeviled, to ask you another question put to me by my Guardian Devil."

"Ask it."

"Yesterday, when you gave me Communion, you asked me to pray for all of us, and even for..."

"That's enough!... Go on."

"I arrived home and began to pray; when I came to the part 'Pray for us sinners, now and at the hour of our death,' a voice in me asked:

'Sinners? Sinners are we? And what is our sin?' What is our sin, Father?"

"Our sin?" he replied. "A great doctor of the Spanish Catholic Apostolic Church has already explained it; the great doctor of *Life is a Dream* has written 'The greatest sin of man is to have been born.' That, my child, is our sin; to have been born."

"Can it be atoned, Father?"

"Go and pray again. Pray once more for us sinners, now and at the hour of our death...Yes, at length the dream is atoned ... at length life is atoned ... at length the cross of birth is expiated and atoned, and the drama comes to an end.... And as Calder6n said, to have done good, to have feigned good, even in dreams, is something which is not lost."

The hour of his death arrived at last.

The entire village saw it come. And he made it his finest lesson: he would not die alone or at rest. He died preaching to his people in the church. But first, before being carried to the church (his paralysis made it impossible for him to move), he summoned Lazarus and me to his bedside. Alone there, the three of us together, he said:

"Listen to me: watch over these poor sheep; find some comfort for them in living, and let them believe what I could not. And Lazarus, when your hour comes, die as I die, as Angela will die, in the arms of the Holy Mother Church, Catholic, Apostolic, and Roman; that is to say, of the Holy Mother Church of Valverde de Lucerna. And now, farewell; until we never meet again, for this dream of life is coming to an end..."

"Father, Father," I cried out.

"Do not grieve, Angela, only go on praying for all sinners, for all who have been born. Let them dream, let them dream ... O, what a longing I have to sleep, to sleep, sleep without end, sleep for all eternity, and never dream! Forgetting this dream!... When they go to bury me, let it be in a box made from the six planks I cut from the old walnut tree—poor old tree!—in whose shade I played as a child, when I began the dream.... In those days, I did really believe in life everlasting. That is to say, it seems to me now that I believed. For a child, to believe is the same as to dream. And for a people, too. ... You'll find those six planks I cut at the foot of the bed."

He was seized by a sudden fit of choking, but composing himself once more, he went on:

"You will recall that when we prayed together, animated by a common sentiment, a community of spirit, and we came to the final verse of the Creed, you will remember that I fell silent.... When the Israelites were coming to the end of their wandering in the desert, the Lord told Aaron and Moses that because they had not believed in Him they would not set foot in the Promised Land with their people; and he bade them climb the heights of Mount Hor, where Moses ordered Aaron stripped of his garments, so that Aaron died there, and then Moses went up from the plains of Moab to Mount Nebo, to the top of Pisgah, looking into Jericho, and the Lord showed him all of the land promised to His people, but said to him: 'You will not go there.' And there Moses died. And no one knew his grave. And he left Joshua to be chief in his place.

"You, Lazarus, must be my Joshua, and if you can make the sun stand still, make it stop, and never mind progress. Like Moses, I have seen the face of God—our supreme dream—face to face, and as you already know,

53

and as the Scripture says, he who sees God's face, he who sees the eyes of the dream, the eyes with which He looks at us, will die inexorably and forever. And therefore, do not let our people, so long as they live, look into the face of God. Once dead, it will no longer matter, for then they will see nothing ..."

"Father, Father, Father," I cried again.

And he said:

"Angela, you must pray always, so that all sinners may go on dreaming, until they die, of the resurrection of the flesh and the life everlasting ..."

I was expecting "and who knows it might be. . ." But instead, Don Manuel had another attack of coughing.

"And now," he finally went on, "and now, in the hour of my death, it is high time to have me brought, in this very chair, to the church, so that I may take leave there of my people, who await me.

He was carried to the church and brought, in his armchair, into the chancel, to the foot of the altar. In his hands he held a crucifix. My brother and I stood close to him, but the fool Blasillo wanted to stand even closer. He wanted to grasp Don Manuel by the hand, so that he could kiss it. When some of the people nearby tried to stop him, Don Manuel rebuked them and said:

"Let him come closer.... Come, Blasillo, give me your hand."

The fool cried for joy. And then Don Manuel spoke:

"I have very few words left, my children; I scarcely feel I have strength enough left to die. And then, I have nothing new to tell you, either. I have already said everything I have to say. Live with each other in peace and contentment, in the hope that we will all see each other again someday, in that other Valverde de Lucerna up there among the nighttime stars, the stars which the lake reflects over the image of the reflected mountain. And pray, pray to the Most Blessed Mary, and to our Lord. Be good... that is enough. Forgive me whatever wrong I may have done you inadvertently or unknowingly. After I give you my blessing, let us pray together, let us say the Paternoster, the Ave Maria, the Salve, and the Creed."

Then he gave his blessing to the whole village, with the crucifix held in his hand, while the women and children cried and even some of the men wept softly.

Almost at once the prayers were begun. Don Manuel

listened to them in silence, his hand in the hand of Blasillo the fool, who began to fall asleep to the sound of the praying. First the Paternoster, with its "Thy will be done on earth as it is in heaven;" then the Ave Maria, with its "Pray for us sinners, now and in the hour of our death;" followed by the Salve, with its "mourning and weeping in this vale of tears;" and finally, the Creed. On reaching "The resurrection of the flesh and life everlasting," the people sensed that their saint had given his soul to God. It was not necessary to close his eyes even, for he died with them closed.

When an attempt was made to wake Blasillo, it was found that he, too, had fallen asleep in the Lord forever. So that later there were two bodies to be buried.

The village immediately repaired en masse to the house of the saint to carry away holy relics, to divide up pieces of his garments among themselves, to carry off whatever they could find as a memento of the blessed martyr. My brother preserved his breviary, between the pages of which he discovered a carnation, dried as in a herbarium and mounted on a piece of paper, and upon the paper a cross and a certain date.

No one in the village believed that Don Manuel was dead; everyone expected to see him—perhaps some of them did—taking his daily walk along the side of the lake, his figure mirrored in the water, or silhouetted against the background of the mountain. They continued to hear his voice, visiting his grave around which a veritable cult sprang up. Old women "possessed by devils" came to touch the cross of walnut, made with his own hands from the tree which had yielded the six planks of his casket.

The ones who least of all believed in his death were my brother and I. Lazarus carried on the tradition of the saint, and he began to compile a record of the priest's words. Some of the conversations in this account of mine were made possible by his notes.

"It was he," said my brother, "who made me into a new man. I was a true Lazarus whom he raised from the dead. He gave me faith."

"Ah, faith ..."

"Yes, faith, faith in the charity of life, in life's joy. It was he who cured me of my delusion of 'progress,' of my belief in its political implications. For there are, Angela, two types of dangerous and harmful men: those who, convinced of life beyond the grave, of the resurrection of the flesh, torment other people—like the inquisitors they are—so that they will despise this life as a transitory thing and work for the other life; and then, there are those who, believing only in this life ..."

"Like you, perhaps ..."

"Yes, and like Don Manuel. Believing only in this world, this second group looks forward to some vague future society and exerts every effort to prevent the populace finding consoling joy from belief in another world ..."

"And so ..."

"The people should be allowed to live with their illusion."

The poor priest who came to the parish to replace Don Manuel found himself overwhelmed in Valverde de Lucerna by the memory of the saint, putting himself in the hands of my brother and myself for guidance. He wanted only to follow in the footsteps of the saint. And my brother told him: "Very little theology, Father, very little theology. Religion, religion, religion." Listening to him, I smiled to myself, wondering if this was not a kind of

58

theology, too.

I now feared for my poor brother. From the time Don Manuel died it could scarcely be said that he lived. Daily he went to the priest's tomb; for hours on end he stood gazing into the lake filled with nostalgia for deep, and abiding peace.

"Don't stare into the lake so much," I begged him.

"Don't worry. It's not this lake which draws me, nor the mountain. Only, I cannot live without his help."

"And the joy of living, Lazarus, what about the joy of living?"

"That's for others. Not for those of us who have *seen* God's face, those of us on whom the Dream of Life has gazed with His eyes."

"What; are you preparing to go and see Don Manuel?"

"No, sister, no. Here at home now, between the two of us, the whole truth—bitter as it may be, bitter as the sea into which the sweet waters of our lake flow—the whole truth for you, who are so set against it. . ."

"No, no, Lazarus. You are wrong. Your truth is not the truth."

"It's my truth."

"Yours, perhaps, but surely not. .."

"His, too."

"No, Lazarus. Not now, it isn't. Now, he must believe otherwise; now he must believe . . ."

"Listen, Angela, once Don Manuel told me that there are truths which, though one reveals them to oneself, must be kept from others; and I told him that telling me was the same as telling himself. And then he said, he confessed to me, that he thought that more than one of the great saints, perhaps the very greatest himself, had died without believing in the other life."

"Is it possible?"

"All too possible! And now, sister, you must be careful that here, among the people, no one even suspects our secret..."

"Suspect it?" I cried in amazement. "Why even if I were to try, in a fit of madness, to explain it to them, they wouldn't understand it. The people do not understand your words, they understand your actions much better. To try and explain all this to them would be like reading some pages from Saint Thomas Aquinas to eight-year-old children, in Latin."

"All the better. In any case, when I am gone, pray for me and for him and for all of us."

At length, his own time came. A sickness which had been eating away at his robust nature seemed to flare with the death of Don Manuel.

"I don't so much mind dying" he said to me in his last days, "as the fact that with me another piece of Don Manuel dies too. The remainder of him must live on with you. Until, one day, even we dead will die forever."

When he lay in the throes of death, the people of the village came in to bid him farewell (as is customary in our towns) and they commended his soul to the care of Don Manuel Bueno, Martyr. My brother said nothing to them; he had nothing more to say. He had already said everything there was to say. He had become a link between the two Valverde de Lucernas—the one at the bottom of the lake and the one reflected in its surface. He was already one more of us who had died of life, and, in his way, one more of our saints.

I was desolate, more than desolate.

But I was, at least, among my own people, in my own village. Now, having lost my San Manuel, the father of

61

my soul, and my own Lazarus, my more than carnal brother, my spiritual brother—I realize that I have aged. But, have I really lost them then? Have I grown old? Is my death approaching?

I must live! And he taught me to live, he taught us to live, to feel life, to feel the meaning of life, to merge with the soul of the mountain, with the soul of the lake, with the soul of the village, to lose ourselves in them so as to remain in them forever. He taught me by his life to lose myself in the life of the people of my village, and I no longer felt the passing of the hours, and the days, and the years, any more than I felt the passage of the water in the lake.

It seemed to me hat my life would always be thus. I no longer felt myself growing old. I no longer lived in myself, but in my people, and my people lived in me. I tried to speak as they spoke, as they spoke without trying. I went into the street—it was the one highway—and, since I knew everyone, I lived in them and forgot myself (while, on the other hand, in Madrid, where I went once with my brother, I had felt a terrible loneliness, since I knew no one, and had been tortured by the sight of so many unknown people).

Now, as I write this memoir, this confession of my experience with saintliness, with a saint, I am of the opinion that Don Manuel Bueno, my Don Manuel, and my brother, too, died believing they did not believe, but that, without believing in their belief, they actually believed, with resignation and in desolation.

But why, I have asked myself repeatedly, did not Don Manuel attempt to convert my brother deceitfully, with a lie, pretending to be a believer himself without being one? And I have finally come to think that Don Manuel realized he would not be able to delude him, that with him a fraud would not do, that only through the truth, with his truth, would he be able to convert him; that he knew he would accomplish nothing if he attempted to enact the comedy— the tragedy, rather—which he played out for the benefit of the people.

And he won him over, in effect, to his pious fraud; thus did he win him over to the cause of life with the truth of death.

And thus did he win me; he who never permitted anyone to see through his divine, his most saintly game. For I believed then, and I believe now, that God—as part of I know not what sacred and inscrutable purpose—caused them to believe they were unbelievers. And that at the moment of their passing, perhaps, the blindfold was removed.

And I, do I believe?

As I write this—here in my mother's old house, and I past my fiftieth year and my memories growing as dim and blanched as my hair, outside it is snowing, snowing upon the lake, snowing upon the mountain, upon the memory of my father, the stranger, upon the memory of my mother, my brother Lazarus, my people, upon the memory of my San Manuel, and even on the memory of the poor fool Blasillo, my Saint Blasillo—and may he help me in heaven! The snow effaces corners and blots out shadows, for even in the night it shines and illuminates. Truly, I do not know what is true and what is false, nor what I saw and what I merely dreamt—or rather, what I dreamt and what I merely saw—, nor what I really knew or what I merely believed true. Neither do I know whether or not I am transferring to this paper, white as the snow outside, my consciousness, for it to remain in writing, leaving me without it. But why, any longer, cling to it?

Do I really understand any of it? Do I really believe in

any of it? Did what I am writing about here actually take place, and did it take place in just the way I tell it? Is it possible for such things to happen? Is it possible that all this is more than a dream dreamed within another dream? Can it be that I, Angela Carballino, a woman in her fifties, am the only one in this village to be assailed by far-fetched thoughts, thoughts unknown to everyone else? And the others, those around me, do they believe? And what does it mean, to believe? At least they go on living. And now they believe in San Manuel Bueno, Martyr, who with no hope of immortality for himself, preserved their hope in it.

Our most illustrious bishop, who set in motion the process for beatifying our saint from Valverde de Lucerna, is intent on writing an account of Don Manuel's life, something which would serve as a guide for the perfect parish priest, and with this end in mind he is gathering information of every sort. He has repeatedly solicited information from me, having more than once come to see me; and I have supplied him with all sorts of facts. But I have never revealed the tragic secret of Don Manuel and my brother. And it is curious that he has never suspected. I trust that what I have set down here will never come to his knowledge. For, all temporal authorities are to be avoided; I fear all authorities on this earth—even when they are church authorities.

But this is an end to it. Let its fate be what it will...

## Epilogue

How, you ask, did this document, this memoir of Angela Carballino fall into *my* hands? That, reader, is something I must keep secret. I have transcribed it for you just as it is written, just as it came to me, with only a few, a very few editorial emendations. Does it remind you other things I have written? This fact does not gainsay its objectivity, its originality. Moreover, for all I know, perhaps I created real, actual beings, independent of me, beyond my control, characters with immortal souls. For all I know, Augusto Perez in my novel *Mist* was right when he claimed to be more real, more objective than I myself, who had thought to have invented him. As for the reality of this —as he is revealed to me by his disciple and spiritual daughter Angela Carballino—of his reality it has not occurred to me to doubt. I believe in it more than the saint himself did. I believe in it more than I do in my own reality.

And now, before I bring this epilogue to a close, I

wish to recall to your mind, patient reader, the ninth verse of the Epistle of the forgotten Apostle, Saint Judas—what power in a name!—where we are told how my heavenly patron, St. Michael Archangel (Michael means "Who such as God?" and archangel means arch-messenger) disputed with the Devil (Devil means accuser, prosecutor) over the body of Moses, and would not allow him to carry it off as a prize, to damnation. Instead, he told the Devil: "May the Lord rebuke thee." And may he who wishes to understand, understand!

I would like also, since Angela Carballino injected her own feelings into her narrative—I don't know how it could have been otherwise— to comment on her statement to the effect that if Don Manuel and his disciple Lazarus had confessed their convictions to the people, they, the people, would not have understood. Nor, I should like to add, would they have believed the pair. They would have believed in their works and not their words. And works stand by themselves, and need no words to back them up. In a village like Valverde de Lucerna one makes one's confession by one's conduct.

And as for faith, the people scarcely know what it is,

67

and can care less.

I am well aware fact that no action takes place in this narrative: this *novelistic* narrative. If you will, the novel is after all the most intimate, the truest history, so that I scarcely understand why some people are outraged to have the Bible called a novel, when such a designation actually sets it above some mere chronicle or other.

In short, nothing happens.

But I hope that this is because everything that takes place happens, and, instead of coming to pass, and passing away, remains forever —like the lakes and the mountains and the blessed simple souls fixed firmly beyond faith and despair— the blessed souls who, in the lakes and the mountains, outside history— in their divine novel, take refuge.

SALAMANCA, 1930